Looking for Alex

Contents

Looking for Alex

Marian Iseard

Published in association with
The Basic Skills Agency

Hodder

A MEMBER OF THE

Acknowledgements
Cover: Stephanie Hawken
Illustrations: Jim Eldridge

Orders; please contact Bookpoint Ltd, 39 Milton Park, Abingdon, Oxon OX14 4TD. Telephone: (44) 01235 400414, Fax: (44) 01235 400454. Lines are open from 9.00–6.00, Monday to Saturday, with a 24 hour message answering service. Email address: orders@bookpoint.co.uk

British Library Cataloguing in Publication Data
A catalogue record for this title is available from the British Library

ISBN 0 340 77614 5

First published 2000
Impression number 10 9 8 7 6 5 4 3 2 1
Year   2005 2004 2003 2002 2001 2000

Copyright © 2000 Marian Iseard

Typeset by GreenGate Publishing Services, Tonbridge, Kent.
Printed in Great Britain for Hodder and Stoughton Educational, a division of Hodder Headline Plc, 338 Euston Road, London NW1 3BH, by Atheneum Press, Gateshead, Tyne & Wear

1

Best Friends

Alex is my best friend.
We had met on our first day
at Newfield Comp.
We sat together,
and we've been friends ever since,
even though we've left school now.

When we were at school
we used to talk about all the things
we'd do when we left.

'We'll get a job, save some money –
go on great holidays.'
You know – the usual stuff.

Alex couldn't wait to leave home.
Me, I didn't mind so much.
I mean, Mum and I shout at each other
sometimes, and my kid brother, Sean,
gets on my nerves. But we get on okay really.

Alex was unhappy at home.
She said her Mum and Dad argued a lot.
Well I suppose that would get you down.
I don't think they had much time for her.

Anyway then we left school.
Alex went onto a training scheme,
working in a shop.
I went to college, doing a computer course.
Alex, though, she kept talking about
moving out.

She said it so often I didn't take any notice.
Maybe I should have done.

2

Alex is Missing

One night Alex's Mum rang,
asking if Alex was with me.
She sounded worried.
She said they hadn't seen Alex
since the morning. No one knew
where Alex was – or who she was with.
I couldn't help, I hadn't seen Alex all day.
I put the phone down and looked
at my watch. Ten-thirty.
Not that late – but why hadn't Alex
said where she was going?

I went to bed wondering what Alex
was playing at, not knowing that
whatever she was up to –
it certainly wasn't a game.

Early the next morning, the doorbell rang.
A policewoman was standing
on the doorstep.

'Are you Louise Thompson?'
I nodded. I couldn't believe
this was happening.
'I'd like to talk to you about your friend Alex.
She seems to have gone missing.'

I answered all the policewoman's questions,
but it was as if I was in a dream.
Until I got to the bit about Alex wanting to
leave home. Then I felt awful.
Like I'd betrayed her.

The policewoman looked very serious
and said that if Alex tried to contact me
I must tell them at once.

After she'd gone I decided I had to
try and find Alex myself.
I thought she might just be
hanging around town,
afraid to go home,
worried that she'd be in trouble.
I didn't say anything to Mum,
she'd only say that I'd be better off at college.

I spent the day going round town,
to all the places we hang out.
I looked in shops, and sat about in cafés,
hoping I'd spot her.

At five o'clock I went home feeling helpless.
I wished and wished that Alex would phone
and say, like she always does, 'Hi! its me!'

I wanted everything to be normal,
for us to laugh about how
we'd all been worried about her.
I just wanted to know where she was.

It was ten o'clock when the phone rang.

I ran to get it. It was Alex's Mum.
Silently I listened as she told me
what the police had found out.
That yesterday Alex had got on the bus
to London – with a single ticket.
She was in tears.
As I put the phone down
I felt like crying myself.

So Alex *had* gone, without telling me,
or anyone. Making everyone so unhappy –
how could she have done it?
Were things really that bad?

3

No News

A week went by, and we heard nothing.
Suddenly one day I knew what I had to do.
I had to go to London myself.

'Don't be daft!' Mum exploded,
when I told her.
'You don't know London!
How could *you* find Alex? You'd get lost!'

I kept on at her, but she wasn't happy.
She said, 'If Alex really wants to disappear,
London's the best place to do it.
It's a big city – you'll never find her.'

But Mum must have seen I was desperate
to do something.
That was when she came up with
one of her bright ideas.

'Auntie Sheila!'
She'd been Mum's best friend at school.
Even so, I didn't get it.
'You know – Eddie.'
Eddie was Sheila's son.
Loud-mouthed, and spotty with it.
'He's two years older than you,
and he's out of work at the moment.
Just left college and looking for a job.'

'So?' I said, knowing what was coming.

'Well, they live in London don't they?
I'm sure Eddie would help you.

Then you'd be happy, looking for Alex
and I'd be happy,
knowing you were safe.'

I won't be happy, I thought,
trailing round with Eddie,
but I could see she had a point.
Mum didn't want *me* to disappear too.
I hugged her tight.
'Thanks Mum.'

4

Eddie

Soon it was all sorted out.
Two days later saw Mum waving me off
at the bus station.
'Be careful!' were her last words –
through the window just as the bus was
starting up.
Now that I was really going
I felt quite scared.

Victoria bus station was a huge place,
full of buses and people with bags.

I thought of Alex,
on her own in this big, strange place.
So many people, so much noise.
How would she have felt,
and where would she have gone?

Forget it, I told myself.
I had to look for Eddie –
but there wasn't a spotty boy in sight.
I put my bags down, and stood watching
a tall, dark-haired guy who was
making his way through the crowds.
He looked nice … and he was heading
this way. It couldn't be … could it?

'Excuse me? Are you Louise?'

I was so surprised that
at first I couldn't speak.

'Eddie?' I said.

'That's me! Don't you remember me?
Here, I'll take your bag. It looks heavy.'

It was amazing.
In three years loud-mouthed Eddie
had changed into this.
It was so brilliant, I wished Alex was here!
Then I remembered that
that's why I was here,
and wiped the silly grin off my face.

We went home by bus –
a real London bus, just like the toy one
I used to play with.
On the way Eddie warned me
about the chances of finding Alex.

'Kids come here all the time,
running away from home.
Most of them end up on the streets.'

'I know. I know all that
but being here is better than being at home.
I just want to be doing something.
You will still help, won't you?'

'Yes. I'll help. Just don't hope for too much.'

I wished everyone wouldn't keep saying that.
Sheila said it too, over dinner.
I knew it was a million to one chance
that I would find Alex – but I still had to try.
I had one photo.
I had Eddie to help –
which was not so bad after all!

5

Going Underground

Eddie had it all planned out.
We seemed to spend all the next day
on the underground.

It was exciting at first.
Hot blasts of air and the squeal of brakes,
people all crowding in together.
And places I'd heard of but would never have
thought I'd go to all in one day.

Eddie laughed at my face
as we waited for tickets.

'You'll soon get fed up with the tube.
By this evening you'll be begging
not to get on another train!'

At the first big station – King's Cross
– we went up to the platforms.

Asking people was hard.
Most people hardly bothered to listen.
Others looked at the photo and
then shook their heads.
One or two looked more closely.
One woman took so long over it
that my heart jumped, but all she said was,
'She looks just like my grand-daughter.'

It was the same everywhere we went.
Nobody really wanted to know.
One man, red in the face and cross,
shouted at me.

'I see hundreds of kids like that every day.
They've all run away.
Why should I know where they go?'

'Don't get upset,' Eddie said to the man.
'This isn't hundreds of kids.
This is one kid and we're trying to find her.'

'Pah! It's a waste of time,' he grunted.

By the evening, as Eddie had said,
I was ready to go home. I was very tired.
I felt like giving up there and then.

'You'll feel better after some food,'
Eddie said. 'Don't look so fed up.
Tomorrow's another day.'

All I could think of was the cross man's words –
'It's a waste of time.'

6

The Streets of London

The week went by.
We went all over London, to all the sights.
We went up and down Oxford Street,
in all the big shops.
Every day that went past I felt
more and more that it was impossible.
We would never find her,
but I didn't say anything.

If I did, maybe Eddie would agree with me,
and want to give up.

One night we went out late,
to places that Eddie knew of,
where the homeless sleep on the streets.
They had shelters made of all sorts –
boxes, bits of plastic, newspaper.
They huddled there in blankets
and thick coats.

Some were as young as me, or younger.
(I tried not to think of Alex sleeping out
like this, it was too awful.)

We talked to some and showed them
Alex's photo, but nobody had seen her.

'We don't even know if she's still here,' I said,
as we sat eating hot-dogs and drinking coffee.
'She might be anywhere.
She might never have stayed in London.'

I suddenly felt so fed up, and almost angry.
For the first time I was angry at Alex,
for what she had done.

'I'm giving up.' I said.
'This is hopeless. There's no point even trying
any more, I may as well go home.'

'Don't do that,' said Eddie.
'Stay till Saturday. That's when
your bus ticket runs out.'

I thought about going home,
and knew that I would miss London.
I had got used to it. I liked the busy feel of it.
And then – I would miss Eddie too.
More than was good for me.
So there was no point thinking about that.
I would have to get used to life without
either Alex or Eddie when I went home.

'OK,' I said.

'Good. Look, I'm just going over to ask
at that soup kitchen. One last try tonight.'

I watched him go over to the people who
stood waiting for a soup handout.
One by one he showed them the photo.
One by one they shook their heads.
A boy at the end of the line took a look while
Eddie was talking to someone else.
He looked again.
Then he turned and started
walking away, fast.

There was something about the way
he had left so suddenly.
Something strange.
I jumped up and ran after him.

7

A Million to One

'You've seen her, haven't you?'
I said as I caught up with him.
'Who?' the boy muttered.
He didn't even stop.
'The girl in that photo.
She's called Alex.
Do you know where she is?'
'I don't know her.
I don't know who you mean.'

He carried on walking, but I grabbed his arm.

'You do know. I can see it on your face.
Please tell me where she is –
you must tell me.'

By this time Eddie had seen what was
going on and had joined me.

'He knows something,' I said to Eddie.
'I know he does.'

The boy – thin, and hungry-looking –
looked from one to the other of us
and then held his hands out.

'Look,' he said, 'she doesn't want
to see anyone.
She doesn't want to go back home.
You're wasting your time.'

'I don't care,' I said.
Although I knew I would if what he said
was true.
The boy nodded his head, slowly.
'All right. This is what I'll do.
I'll go and ask her. You wait here.
What are your names?'

'I'm Louise. Just tell her Louise is here.
And a friend.'

'I'll be back in a few minutes –
I suppose you may as well hear it from her.
Save you walking your legs off.'

He went, quickly, and vanished
down a side street.

'We should have followed him,' said Eddie.

'No. He would have known.
And anyway, I only want to see Alex
if she wants to see me.
Otherwise there's no point.'

We sat down on a bench, to wait.
In less than ten minutes the boy was back.
He waved to us to follow him.

Only then did it sink in –
I had found her.
It was the million to one chance!

8

Alex

The boy stopped in front of a scruffy
blue door and knocked, twice,
then three times. A sort of code I guessed.

The door opened.
Alex was there, on the other side.
She looked terrible – thin and pale.
'Hello Louise,' she said,
but she was looking at the floor, not me.

'Hello Alex.'

The house was a squat, that was clear.
There wasn't much furniture,
and just a two-bar electric fire.
It smelt of damp.

'This is Eddie,' I said. 'He's a friend.'
She nodded at him, and then looked
at the boy who had taken us there.
'This is Pete.'

All the things I'd planned to ask
went out of my mind.
Then Eddie asked Pete for a cup of tea,
and they went off to make it.
I knew that Eddie had done that
so that Alex and I could talk,
but now I didn't know what to say.

'Why did you go, Alex?'
It was really the only thing
I needed to know.

'I don't know,' she said,
looking at me for the first time.
'I mean – not why then.
You see, it was morning,
I was just about to go to work,
but I needed time to think.
Mum and Dad had had
a huge row the night before,
and I was feeling really angry.

On the way out I picked up some money.
It was lying on the side,
and I just picked it up.
I think I was trying to get back at them.
I thought I might go and buy a CD
or something. I don't know.'
She stopped, and looked down.

'Go on,' I said.

'It was a lot of money. Fifty quid.
It was to pay a bill.
Anyway, I walked past the bus station,
and I thought – I've got fifty pounds.
I can go anywhere I want.
So that's what I did.
I went in and asked what time
the bus to London was.
It was the first place I thought of.
In twenty minutes, the man said.
He said I was lucky because there
was only one bus each day.
So I bought a ticket, and got on the bus.'

Alex suddenly laughed.

'Don't look so shocked! I'm fine.
Pete's really nice – I met him in a café.
He told me there was a spare room here.
He lives here with two others –
Kelly and Josh.'

I had to ask.
'Are you and Pete, like … together?'

'No. He's just a friend.'

'Just good friends,' I said, grinning –
it was our joke when we fancied someone
like mad.

Alex laughed and said, 'Honest!'
and then Pete and Eddie came in with the tea.

'That's better,' Eddie said to me.
That's the first time I've seen you
laugh all week!'

9

The Promise

We talked for a long time.
Alex said she was sorry she'd upset everyone
but she didn't want to go back to her old life.

'I can't live there any more,' she said.
'It was driving me mad.
If Mum and Dad can't live together
they should do something about it.'

'Well you can't stay here,' I said.
'Not forever. It may be all right for a time.

It's an adventure. I can see that.
But you'll get ill.
How do you get money for food?'

She went red.
'The others take care of that.'
Eddie gave me a look.
Was he thinking the same as me?
That they stole it?

We stayed until very late.
Alex said 'Promise me something.
Don't tell anyone. Not yet.'
I knew it would be hard to keep
but I gave her a big hug and said, 'Promise.'

The next day we went back. I was hoping
she'd come home with us this time.
Pete opened the door.
He had an odd look on his face.

'This is for you,' he said,
and handed me a letter.

Dear Louise

I'm sorry to do this to you,
but I couldn't face seeing you again.
I knew you'd make me want to go back home,
and I can't – not yet.
I want to see Mum and Dad again,
but not until I've had some time away from them.
They need to sort their lives out,
and I'd rather not be around while they do it.
Don't worry about me, I'll be all right.
I'm going to try and get a job,
just something to keep me going.
I know what you thought,
the other night, I saw your faces.
Well I won't be living off the others any more,
on food that they've stolen.
I'll pay for things somehow.
I'll write, Louise, I promise.
And I will phone my parents,
so they know I'm safe.
See you.

Love Alex

'We're moving to another place,'
said Pete, when I'd finished
reading the letter, and passed it to Eddie.
I didn't bother asking where.
I knew he wouldn't say.
I told him to give Louise my love,
and we went.

It's funny, but I wasn't upset.
I'd done what I'd set out to do.
I'd found Alex, but if she wouldn't
come back – well, that was up to her.
And, in finding Alex, I'd found Eddie.
Somehow knowing Eddie made a difference.
Not that Alex was any less important,
and I might never see Eddie again.
But somehow things had changed.

Back at Sheila's we found that Alex
had already phoned home.
Everyone wanted to talk to me –
including the police.
By bedtime I was all talked out,
too tired to think any more.

10

Going Home

The next day was Saturday.
My bus left at eleven o'clock.
We got to the bus station in good time,
and had a cup of tea in the café.
'What will you do now?' asked Eddie.
'Go back to college,' I said.
'I'll have to catch up on my work.
Then there's exams. What about you?'

'Oh, carry on looking for a job. This week's
been a nice rest from writing letters.'

'Well you'll have to write *me* a letter now,'
I said, and then could have kicked myself.
My face was going hot. I stood up
and picked up my bag.
'I think I'd better get a seat on the bus,' I said.

At the bus stand I turned to Eddie and said,
'Thanks for all your help.
I'd never have found Alex without you.'

He smiled, and gave me a kiss on the cheek.
Then we heard the bus starting up
and I rushed to get onto it.

The bus was quite full but
I got a seat next to the window.
I sat down and looked for Eddie
but Eddie had disappeared.
Then, as the bus turned I saw him.
He was writing something on
that looked like a white paper bag.
The bus was at the exit now,
waiting to turn onto the busy main road.
Eddie ran over and waved to me.

He held up the paper bag.
It read – *'Can I come up and see you?'*

'Yes,' I shouted, and then remembered
where I was!
Everyone on my side of the bus laughed
and cheered – they'd all read it too!
For the second time that day
I felt my face go red, but this time
I didn't care. As the bus set off,
I whispered to myself,
'Good luck Alex – and thanks
for helping me find Eddie.'